Flossie Crums

and the

Enchanted
Cookie Tree

Other Flossie Crums titles:

Flossie Crums and The Fairies' Cupcake Ball
Flossie Crums and The Royal Spotty Dotty Cake

Flossie Crums

and the Enchanted Cookie Tree

By Helen Nathan

Illustrated by Daryl Stevenson

PAVILION
CHILDREN'S

To Debbie xx Helen

For Ben and Miranda with all my love xxx DS

This edition first published in the United Kingdom in 2011 by
Pavilion Children's Books
10 Southcombe Street
London W14 0RA
An imprint of Anova Books Company Ltd

10 9 8 7 6 5 4 3 2 1

ISBN 9781843651970

Printed by 1010 Printing International Ltd, China

This book can be ordered direct from the publisher at the website: www.anovabooks.com

Have you ever wondered if
fairies eat cookies? Well, let me tell you,
THEY LOVE COOKIES!
And so do I! Do you?

Hiding on every page, is a tiny fairy – see if you can spot one!
Sometimes you might have to look really hard to find
them. Grown ups will often miss them, so
you might have to help.

Hello! I'm Flossie Crums, aged seven and three quarters. I'm just an ordinary girl, but I also happen to be the Royal Baker of the Fairy Kingdom of Romolonia! Ever since I was little I've always made special cakes, but now I bake for the fairies too.

My Family

My Mum

My Dad

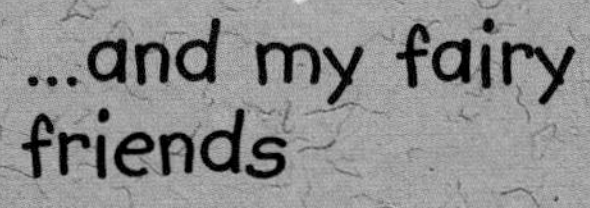

...and my fairy friends

My dog Rocket

My Cat Goliath

My little brother Billie.
He likes collecting bugs... yuck!

I was in my bedroom working on a new recipe—sticky caramel cupcakes—when Billie barged in with his binoculars. He bounced on my bed and yelled,

"Flossie!

Flossie!

There's something **strange** going on in the garden!"

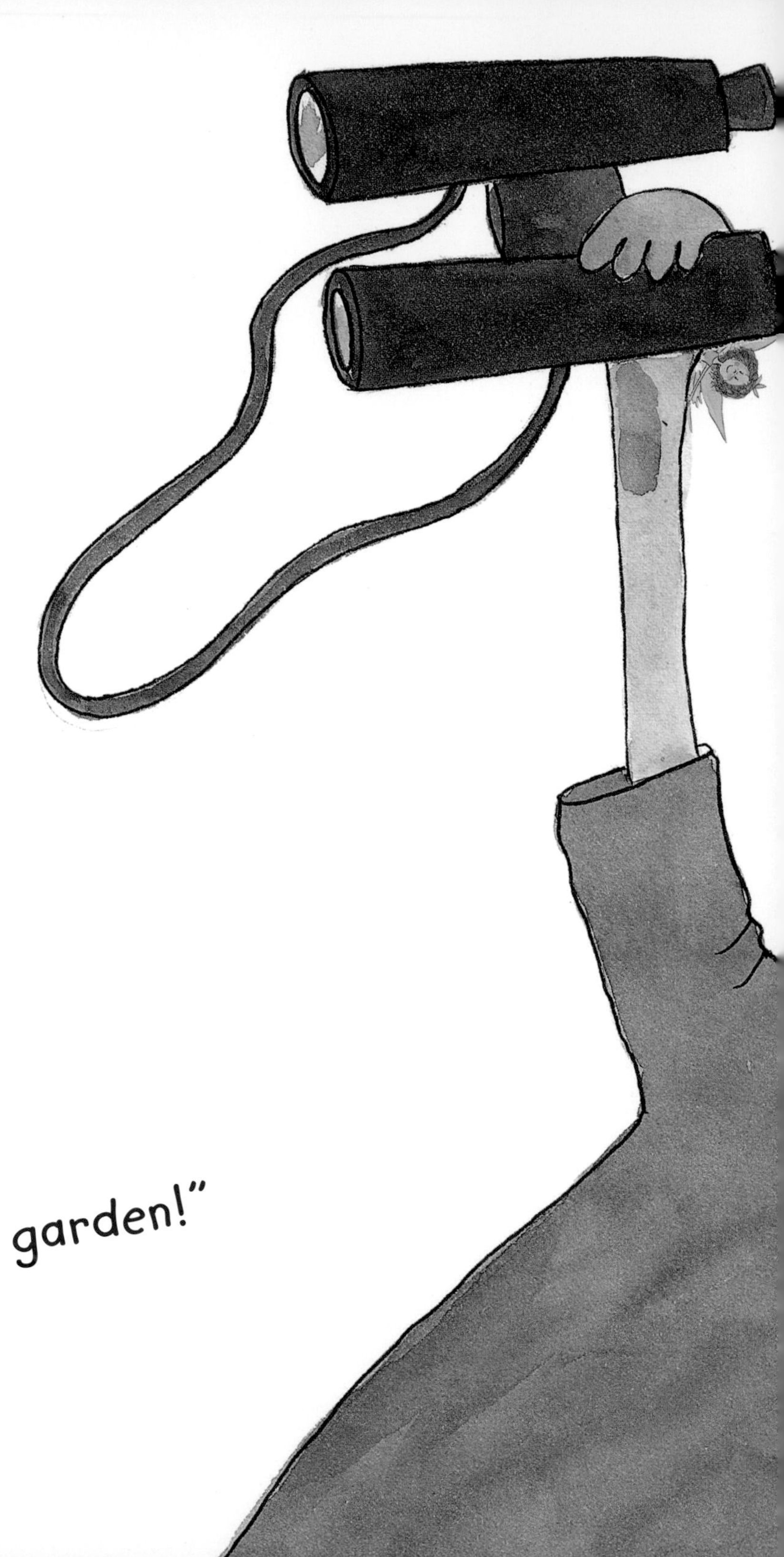

"What?" I said grumpily. "Don't be silly."

I grabbed his binoculars and peered out the window. Sure enough, I could see what he was talking about.

A small twig seemed to be floating across the lawn. Then, I adjusted the binoculars slightly and saw exactly what was happening:

the fairies were back!

Billie and I have **fairies** living in our chestnut tree; a place called the Magical Kingdom of Romolonia.

Billie and I rushed into the garden.
There we found Minty and Honey,
the littlest fairies, struggling to drag
a rather small, leafless branch.
"What on earth are you two doing?" I asked.
"Hi Flossie! Hi Billie! We have found the best tree," Minty beamed.
"Queen Rosie is going to be so proud of us. But we have to wait
until Candy gets here to get back to Romolonia."

Billie bent over and scooped up the branch. The fairies oohed and aahed, fluttering their eyelashes and twittering on about how strong he was. He blushed as they called him Billie the Strong. I raised my eyebrows.

Billie the Strong? Ha!

He dropped the branch by the chestnut tree and said,

"Hate to break it to you, but this isn't really a tree. It's just a tiny bit of one."

"Just you wait and see Billie," said Honey.

"It's the perfect tree for our party!"

"Party?" I asked. "What party?"

"**The Royal Baby Naming Party, of course,**" said Minty.

"A baby naming party!" I cried, clapping my hands.

That meant there was **a new royal baby** in Romolonia!

"Hush!" said Honey.
"It's a secret. We weren't meant to say anything. Candy was. She's the head fairy, after all."
"Don't worry," I said.
"I promise we won't say a thing."
"You better go," said Honey.
"Candy will be here any moment.
Thanks again, Billie the Strong!
We left them sitting on the roots of the chestnut tree, waiting patiently for Candy to arrive.

That night I struggled to sleep, but when I finally drifted off I had the strangest dream. I dreamt I was lying in bed and Minty and Candy were hovering above me, arguing.

"Throw water on her," Minty said. "That'll wake her!"

"No, that's mean. Let's whisper in her ear," Candy suggested.

"I've tried that. She's as deaf as a rock. I'll wiggle her nose a bit."

It felt like a fly had landed on my face, so I swatted it away. And that's when I realised it wasn't a dream. I had just accidentally pushed Minty halfway up my nose.

"Yuck! That's disgusting!" cried Minty. " I've got bogies in my hair!"

"Minty! Candy!" I blinked and rubbed eyes. "You're really here!"

"I have the most exciting news to tell you," said Candy gently.

"Queen Rosie's had a baby girl," she announced formally.

"And she's called Princess Cauliflower," added Minty.

"Not cauliflower, silly," laughed Candy. "Princess Cornflower!"

"A fairy princess," I said dreamily. "I would love to meet her."

"Oh, you will," said Candy. "Queen Rosie wants YOU to make the cookies for the Enchanted Baby Naming Tree."

I couldn't believe I was going to meet a **baby fairy!**

I barely slept the rest of that night. All I could think about was

COOKIES!

I was in the kitchen at the crack of dawn. Not even Rocket and Goliath were awake. They were still curled up together in their basket, snoring.

That morning I sat at the kitchen table drawing cookies, hundreds of them. Then I crept back upstairs and showed them to Billie.

"Mmmmmmm," said Billie.

"They look amazing! Can I make some too?"

Then mum walked in. **"As soon as you've tidied your room,"** she said. **"And not a minute before!"**

"But my room is tidy," said Billie, which was a huge fib. Mum lifted up the duvet and looked under his bed. She found a week's worth of toys and clothes crammed underneath.

Silly Billie! Mum **always** checks under the bed.

I left Billie to tidy his room and followed Mum downstairs. It was time to bake some cookies! Eggs, icing sugar, flour and butter is all you need.

I was just getting another batch out of the oven when a cookie jumped off the rack and walked across the counter!

I picked it up and found a little imp dangling underneath.

He jumped down, ran out the kitchen door and dashed up the stairs.

My Perfect Cookie Recipe

What you need:

200g/7oz/1 cup cold unsalted butter, plus a little extra for the baking tray
280g/10oz/2½ cups plain flour, plus a little extra for rolling out
100g/3½oz/¾ cup icing sugar
2 egg yolks (ask a grown-up to separate the yolks from the whites)

1 tsp vanilla essence
cookie cutters (I used butterflies, prams, dresses, crowns and unicorns but you can use any cutters you have, even the top of a coffee jar would work!)

What you do:

First, make the dough. Use a small knob of butter to grease a 35.5 x 25.5cm/14 x 10 inch baking tray.

Rub the cold butter and flour together in a bowl with your fingertips until the mixture looks like breadcrumbs. Add the icing sugar, egg yolks and vanilla essence and mix well until the dough comes together into a ball. You might think it's too dry and won't work, but use your hands and after a few minutes the butter will soften and help stick everything together. Pop the ball of dough into the fridge for 10 minutes. Ask a grown-up to turn the oven on to 200°C/400°F/gas mark 6.

Sprinkle a handful of flour on the table and a bit on your rolling pin. Roll out the dough. Be sure to wiggle it around so it doesn't stick to the table. If it does, add a bit more flour. Roll it out to 5mm/⅕ inch thick. Get your cutters and stamp out your cookies.

Use a blunt knife to lift the cookies onto your baking tray. You can place the cookies close together because they won't spread while they bake. Ask a grown-up to put the tray in the oven and bake for 12 minutes. When they're done, ask a grown-up to take them out and leave to cool, then transfer to a wire rack.

If you like, take a toothpick and make a hole about 3mm/⅛ inch from the top of the cookies so that you can thread a piece of string or pretty ribbon through to hang them once they're iced. Leave the cookies to cool completely.

Makes 12 large cookies.

Equipment

rolling pin

spatulas and wooden spoons

After the imp incident, things then went from **bad** to **worse.**

To my horror, a **huge black spider** with red spots descended from the kitchen clock and landed on the teapot.

"Hello," he said politely.

"Allow me to introduce myself.
I'm Geoffrey, head of King Saffron's Spyder Security Team.
It appears that some imps have escaped from Romolonia.
We believe that they might be hiding in your house.
Have you seen any?"

A talking spider?

I recovered myself enough to speak.
"Actually, you've just missed one. He tried to run off with one of my cookies! Then he took off up the stairs. He's probably in Billie's room.

"Thank you, madam. I shall go and investigate immediately," said the spider, and he scuttled off in that horrible way that creepy crawlies do.

Thieving imps and talking spiders, **whatever next?!**

While the cookies cooled, I cleaned up the kitchen, as all good bakers do. I was just about to make the icing, when there was an enormous

KERPOOOOF!

It sounded like it came from Billie's room. I ran up the stairs two at a time. Tiny stars and pink smoke seeped out from under the door. Then I heard that horrid spider chanting some sort of spell.

"Laws of goodness
spells of right
magic means and magic might
banish darkness
bring on light
help us put this pig sty right!"

There was a sudden flash. I threw open the door and all of Billie's things flew through the air then neatly landed into their proper place.

"Billie!" I gasped. **"What is going on?"**

"Nothing," said Billie. **"Geoffrey is just helping me tidy my room."**

His room was the tidiest it had ever been, but there was no sign of imps or spiders anywhere. They had disappeared. I shook my head in disbelief, turned around and headed back down to the kitchen to start icing the cookies.

On the next page,
you'll find the
yummiest cookie
icing recipe ever!

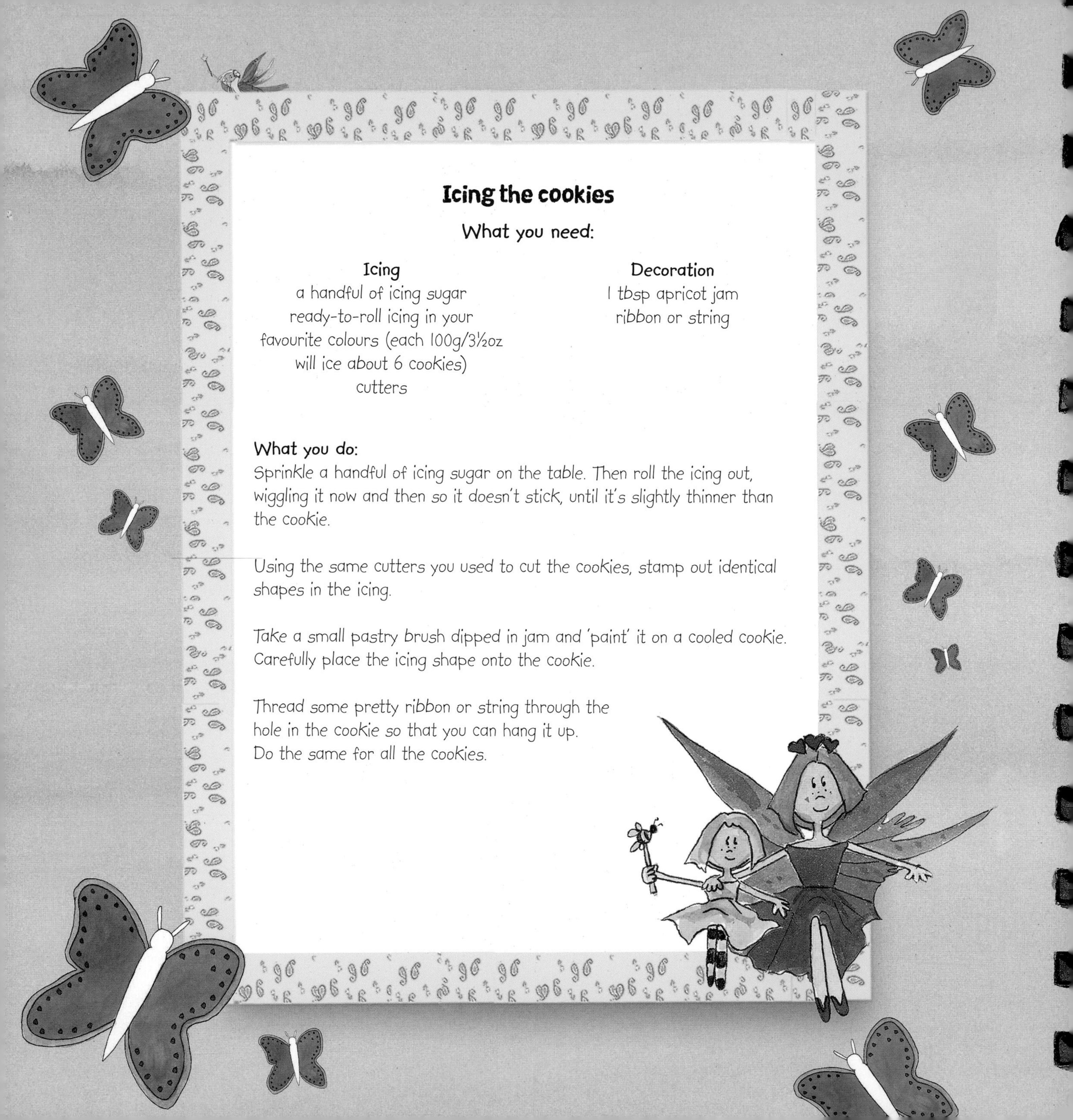

Icing the cookies

What you need:

Icing
a handful of icing sugar
ready-to-roll icing in your favourite colours (each 100g/3½oz will ice about 6 cookies)
cutters

Decoration
1 tbsp apricot jam
ribbon or string

What you do:

Sprinkle a handful of icing sugar on the table. Then roll the icing out, wiggling it now and then so it doesn't stick, until it's slightly thinner than the cookie.

Using the same cutters you used to cut the cookies, stamp out identical shapes in the icing.

Take a small pastry brush dipped in jam and 'paint' it on a cooled cookie. Carefully place the icing shape onto the cookie.

Thread some pretty ribbon or string through the hole in the cookie so that you can hang it up. Do the same for all the cookies.

Butterfly Cookies

What you need:

12 butterfly shaped cookies baked using
My Perfect Cookie Recipe
different coloured ready-to-roll icings
writing icing in different colours
1 tbsp apricot jam

What you do:

Make My Perfect Cookie Recipe, then follow my instructions to ice the cookies using the butterfly cookie cutter.

Very carefully, with brown writing icing, ice little dots all around the edge of each cookie.

To make the butterfly's body, take a small ball of white ready-to-roll icing and, using your fingertips, make a small 'sausage' shape. Glue this into the centre of the cookie witht he jam.

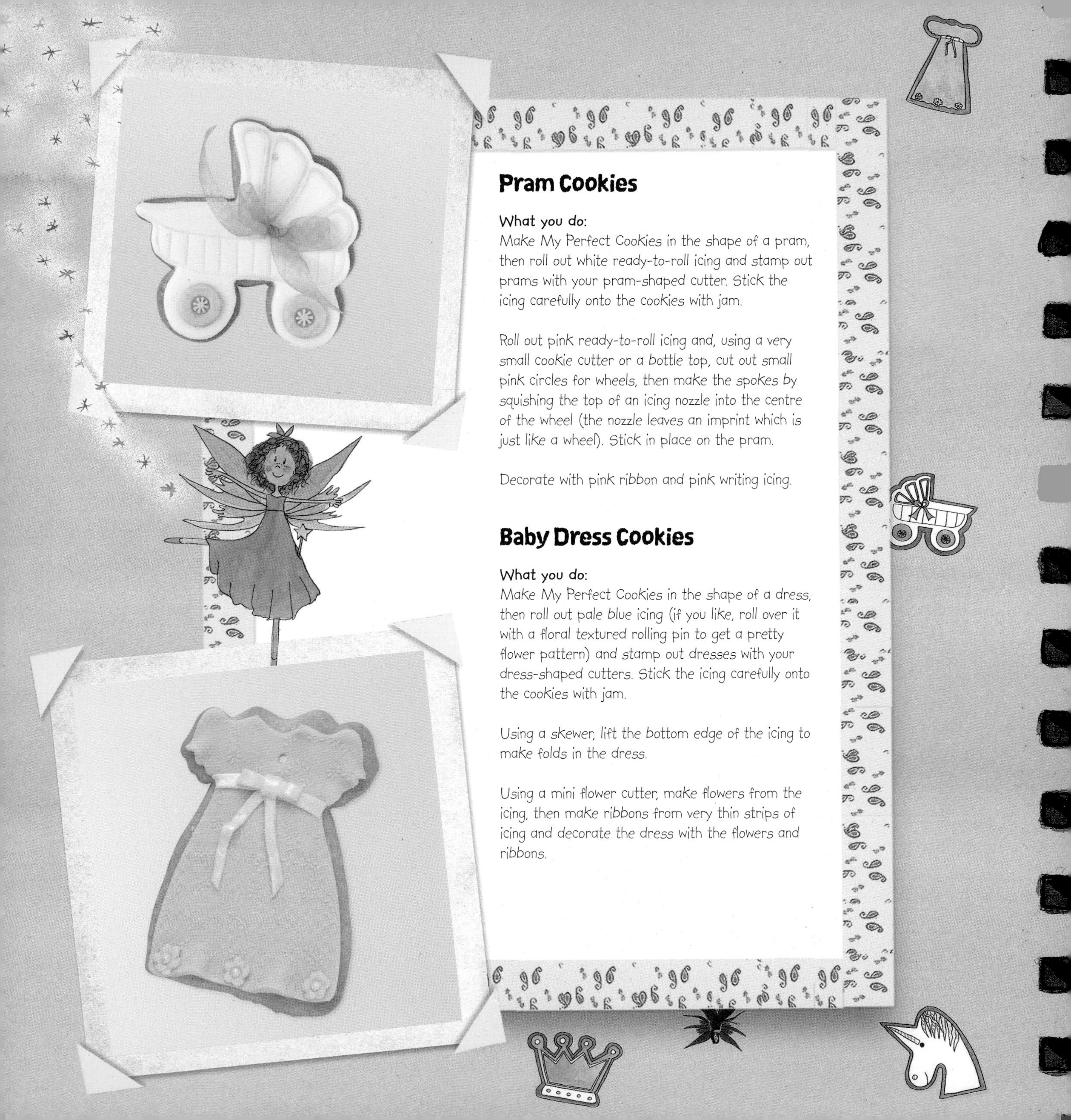

Pram Cookies

What you do:
Make My Perfect Cookies in the shape of a pram, then roll out white ready-to-roll icing and stamp out prams with your pram-shaped cutter. Stick the icing carefully onto the cookies with jam.

Roll out pink ready-to-roll icing and, using a very small cookie cutter or a bottle top, cut out small pink circles for wheels, then make the spokes by squishing the top of an icing nozzle into the centre of the wheel (the nozzle leaves an imprint which is just like a wheel). Stick in place on the pram.

Decorate with pink ribbon and pink writing icing.

Baby Dress Cookies

What you do:
Make My Perfect Cookies in the shape of a dress, then roll out pale blue icing (if you like, roll over it with a floral textured rolling pin to get a pretty flower pattern) and stamp out dresses with your dress-shaped cutters. Stick the icing carefully onto the cookies with jam.

Using a skewer, lift the bottom edge of the icing to make folds in the dress.

Using a mini flower cutter, make flowers from the icing, then make ribbons from very thin strips of icing and decorate the dress with the flowers and ribbons.

Unicorn Cookies

What you do:
Make My Perfect Cookies in the shape of a unicorn, then roll out white ready-to-roll icing and stamp out unicorns with your unicorn-shaped cutter. Stick the icing carefully onto the cookies with jam.

Use black writing icing to draw an eye. Roll lots of little mini sausage shapes out of white icing and stick them on to make a mane.

Finally, roll a small strip of icing to form a unicorn's horn, then glue in place with jam and sprinkle with edible glitter.

Princess Crown Cookies

What you do:
Make My Perfect Cookies in the shape of a crown, then roll out pink ready-to-roll icing and stamp out crowns with your crown-shaped cutter. Stick the icing carefully onto the cookies with jam.

Make or buy very small icing roses for the tips of the crown and stick on using jam.

Cut a strip of white icing and decorate with silver balls, then stick this onto the base of the crown.

Finally, I used a bit of pink edible glitter to make it extra sparkly!

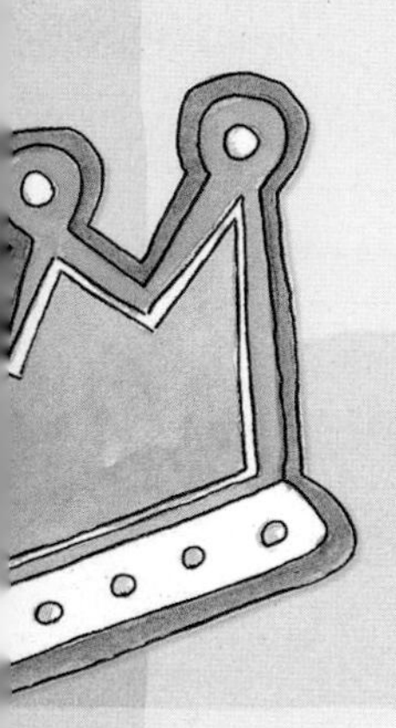

Now that his room was tidy, Billie was allowed to come down and help me ice the cookies. As we decorated the cookies, we talked about Romolonia. He reminded me of my promise: if I were ever invited again, he could come too. So, when he saw Candy fly in, he hopped around the kitchen with excitement.

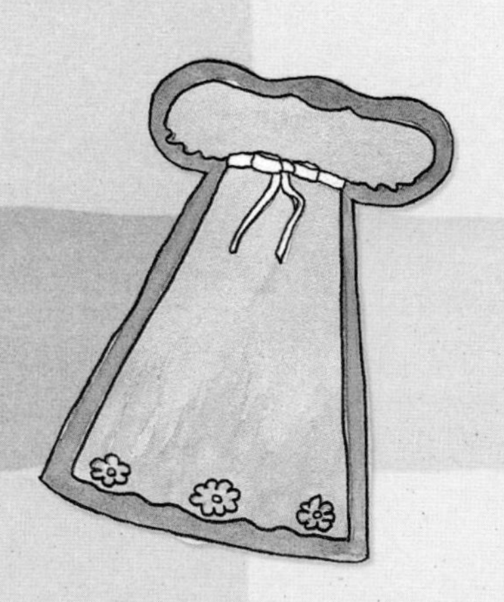

"Oh they are so beautiful!"
she said, admiring our creations. "But we must hurry.
We can't possibly keep the Royal Family waiting."

Billie and I picked up the trays
and Candy waved her magic wand.

"Oh Floss, will we be okay?"
Billie asked as Candy flew around us.
"What if I never get big again?"

"We'll be fine, Billie. I promise.
This is a real adventure.
We're going to Romolonia!"

Billie, Candy and I walked to the chestnut tree, but we were so small it took forever. The garden seemed to be miles long. We couldn't run because we had all the cookies to carry and we didn't have wings so—of course—we couldn't fly.

"We're going to be late," Candy said. "I just don't want to disappoint King Saffron and Queen Rosie. This is so important to them."

I was worried, too. I didn't want to let them down either, so I walked faster. Just as we reached the tree, the door opened and out fluttered Cherry.

"King Saffron has sent Queen Rosie's magical flying carriage," she announced.
We wouldn't be late, after all! We all hopped in and were whisked off to the palace.

We had a wonderful view of Romolonia as we soared through the sky. It was so magical it took my breath away. I pointed out to Billie the lemonade river and the marshmallow meadows and all the other wonderful sights. Up head stood the ice cream palace.

"Wow! Look at that," Billie squeaked as we landed outside the palace

Cherry and Candy guided us down a long corridor then stopped in front of a giant shimmering door. **"The Icicle Ballroom,"** announced Candy.

"All royal babies have their naming ceremony here."

The door opened and everyone inside turned and cheered.

Billie and I couldn't stop staring! Diamond studded icicles hung from the ceiling making the room twinkle and glisten.

King Saffron and Queen Rosie stood proudly beside a snowflake crib, where the baby lay wrapped up, cozy and warm. Behind them stood the branch Billie had helped the fairies carry. But it wasn't little any more.

It was **ENORMOUS!**

One by one the fairies came forward, chose a cookie and flew to the Enchanted Tree, where they hung it on a branch.

When all the cookies were on the tree, Honey carried a purple cushion with a silver heart resting on it to Queen Rosie.

"That's the magic silver heart," whispered Candy. "Watch what happens next."

Queen Rosie lifted the silver heart from the cushion and suddenly the giant tree began to shake. I thought the magic had begun, but it wasn't magic.

Having spied the delicious treats on the tree, a band of naughty imps swarmed the icicle ballroom. They were stealing princess Cornflower's naming cookies.

This was a disaster!

"Arrest those imps!" thundered King Saffron.

The Spyder Security Team raced up the tree in pursuit of the thieves. The tree shook violently. It wavered, and then it started to fall...

right in the path of the Royal Family.

Everyone gasped. We were all too shocked to move. But not Billie! He grabbed Queen Rosie's wand and spoke very quickly.

"Laws of goodness
spells of right
stand this naming tree upright!"

The tree stopped in mid-air. Then, instead of crushing the Royal Family, it returned to its original position.

PHEW! For a few seconds there was complete silence, and then everyone clapped and shouted.

Billie, my clever little brother, had saved the day!

Geoffrey then led the naughty imps away in handcuffs. Everything was right again.

Queen Rosie turned to Billie and beckoned him forward.

"We have heard about your strength," she said. **"But you are brave, too."**

She waved her wand and a gold medal appeared around Billie's neck.

"From now on you shall be known as Sir Billie the Brave."

Billie looked like he might burst with pride.

Queen Rosie stepped back and picked up the silver heart. She flew into the air and placed the heart on top of the Enchanted Tree... then the tree shuddered.

Oh no, not again!

But this time each of the branches sparkled and glimmered, until the whole tree shimmered like diamonds. Just when I thought it couldn't get any more beautiful, silver fireworks exploded above us, lighting up the Icicle Ballroom in a silvery shower.

Princess
Cornflower

Queen Rosie took the baby from the crib. **"Use your magic well,"** she said smiling and holding the baby to face the tree.

The baby laughed and gurgled, and then I gasped as two tiny wings sprouted from her back.

The Queen turned to face the crowd.

"I name this baby Princess Cornflower.
May she help rule Romolonia with kindness and love."

And then she added, **"Before this ceremony ends,**
I would like to thank Flossie Crums, for making
the wonderful cookies for the Enchanted Tree.
Three cheers to our Royal Baker of Romolonia!"

Hip-hip hurray!

Hip-hip hurray! Hip-hip hurray!

I blushed. I didn't want to leave Romolonia,
but I knew it was time to go back home.

Billie stared at his medal.
"I wish we could stay here," he said sadly.
"I won't be Sir Billie the Brave when I get home."

"Yes you will," I said. **"You'll be Sir Billie the Brave**
wherever you go. You have your medal to prove it."

Plum and Cherry led us back to the magic door and, once we were outside, Plum flew around us until we were our normal size again.

In the kitchen, Mum was still tidying up. You should have seen her face when we told her about the imps in the tree. Then Billie showed her his medal and she nearly fainted!

Later that evening when mum said goodnight, I couldn't help asking her,

"Do you think I'll be going back to Romolonia?"

Mum smiled. **"It seems the fairies really love their Royal Baker. I have a feeling another adventure is just around the corner."**

I have to go now, but I couldn't say goodbye without sharing a few more recipes with you from our adventure in Romolonia. Can you spot where I got my ideas from?

Don't forget to wash your hands and put your apron on. Now, turn the page and start baking!

MARSHMALLOW SPIDER COOKIES

Geoffrey was thrilled to see his very own recipe.

Marshmallow Spider Cookies

What you need:

Cookies

225g/8oz/2 cups plain flour
50g/2oz/½ cup cocoa powder
200g/7oz/1 cup butter
2 egg yolks (ask a grown-up to separate the yolks from the whites)
100g/3½oz/¾ cup icing sugar

Decorations

1 packet red strawberry laces
12 chocolate marshmallow teacakes
apricot jam
chocolate vermicelli
1 packet ready-to-roll white icing
1 tube black writing icing
1 packet ready-to-roll black icing

What you do:

Ask a grown-up to turn the oven on to 200°C/400°F/gas mark 6.

Follow the instructions for making the dough for My Perfect Cookie Recipe but use the ingredients above. Or you could just buy biscuits and have fun with the decorations; however, the chocolate biscuit recipe IS delicious!

Stamp out round cookies and put them on the baking tray. Ask a grown-up to put them in the oven and bake the biscuits for 8 minutes. When they're done, ask a grown-up to take them out the oven and leave them to cool.

To decorate, cut each lace into about 3cm/1¼ inch legs. You'll need 96 legs!

Using a pastry brush, paint the teacakes with jam and sprinkle on the chocolate vermicelli. Next, spread a bit of jam onto each cooled cookie and put a teacake on top to form the spider's body.

Using a skewer, make eight little holes, four on either side of the teacake. Then, take eight lace legs and thread them into the holes to form the spider's legs.

Roll little balls of white ready-to-roll icing to make googly eyes and stick them onto the spider's body. Dot with black writing icing in the middle of each eye.
Make a mouth using some black ready-to-roll icing and glue in place with jam.

Makes about 12 spider cookies.

GLITTERING ICE PALACE COOKIES WITH COCONUT AND WHITE CHOCOLATE

If you hate coconut, like Billie does, just leave it out.

Glittering Ice Palace Cookies with Coconut and White Chocolate

What you need:

Cookies

115g/3¾oz/½ cup softened butter, plus a little extra for the baking tray
115g/3¾oz/½ cup caster sugar
2 tbsp condensed milk
150g/5oz/1⅓ cups self-raising flour
75g/3oz white chocolate chunks
50g/2oz/⅔ cup desiccated coconut

Decorations

2 tbsp caster sugar
white edible glitter (if you've got some)

What you do:

Ask a grown-up to turn the oven on to 180°C/350°F/gas mark 4. Use a small knob of butter to grease two 40.5cm/16 inch baking trays.

Beat the butter and sugar together in a mixing bowl until it's all mixed together and there are no lumpy bits, then stir in the condensed milk.

Add the flour, white chocolate and coconut and then work the mixture into a soft dough. You'll have to use your hands, so make sure they're clean!

Break off small pieces of dough (about the size of a ping-pong ball) and place on the baking trays. Squish the cookies down a little on the tray.

Ask a grown-up to put the tin in the oven and bake for 12–15 minutes or until the edges are slightly golden. When they're done, ask a grown-up to take them out of the oven and leave them to cool on the tray. Once cool, carefully transfer them to a wire rack.

Dust with caster sugar, then sprinkle with white edible glitter, if you've got some.

Makes 12 cookies.

MINI FOOTPRINT BABY CAKES

These mini cakes are just as cute as Princess Cornflour herself

Mini Footprint Baby Cakes

What you need:

Mini-Cakes

55g/2oz/½ cup self-raising flour
1 dsp milk
55g/2oz/¼ cup caster sugar
1 egg
55g/2oz/¼ cup softened butter
1 packet of mini cake cases

Icing and decoration

200g/7oz/1⅔ cups icing sugar
2 tbsp fresh lemon juice
2 dsp water
mini icing baby footprints or you could use pink or blue sweeties

What you do:

Ask a grown-up to turn the oven on to 190°C/375°F/gas mark 5. Place 24 mini-cake cases onto a baking sheet.

Mix all the mini-cake ingredients together in a bowl with a wooden spoon until the batter is smooth and there are no lumpy bits. When the batter is well mixed, spoon 1 teaspoon of mixture into each paper case.

Ask a grown-up to put the tin in the oven and bake for 15 minutes. When they're done, ask a grown-up to take them out. and let the cakes cool completely.

Mix the icing sugar, lemon juice and water together to make a smooth paste, then spread ½ teaspoon of icing onto each cake. Place two tiny feet or sweeties on each cake.

Makes 24 baby cakes.

22 MAPLE SYRUP LANE
CUPCAKES WITH MAPLE ICING

All kinds of cupcake cases are available. Or you can even make your own!

22 Maple Syrup Lane Cupcakes with Maple Icing

What you need:

Cupcakes

115g/3¾oz/1 cup self-raising flour
115g/3¾oz/1 cup softened butter
100g/3½oz/just under ½ cup caster sugar
2 eggs
1 tbsp milk
re-usable picket fence
cupcake wrappers

Icing and decoration

400g/14oz/3¼ cups icing sugar
50g/2oz/¼ cup melted butter
4 tbsp maple syrup
1 dsp cold water
edible flowers, bugs or numbers

What you do:

Ask a grown-up to turn the oven on to 190°C/375°F/gas mark 5. Place 12 cupcake cases in a 12-hole cupcake tin.

Mix all the cupcake ingredients together in a bowl using a wooden spoon. Make sure there are no lumpy bits. When the batter is well mixed, spoon the mixture into the cupcake cases using a dessertspoon.

Ask a grown-up to put the tin in the oven and bake for 18 minutes. When they're done, ask a grown-up to take them out and leave to cool.

Make the icing by mixing the icing sugar, melted butter, maple syrup and cold water together in a bowl until it looks a bit like custard. Spread or pipe a large teaspoon of icing onto each cake and decorate with edible flowers or bugs and numbers.

Makes 12 cupcakes.

PRINCESS CORNFLOWER'S PINK MERINGUE KISSES WITH ROSE CREAM

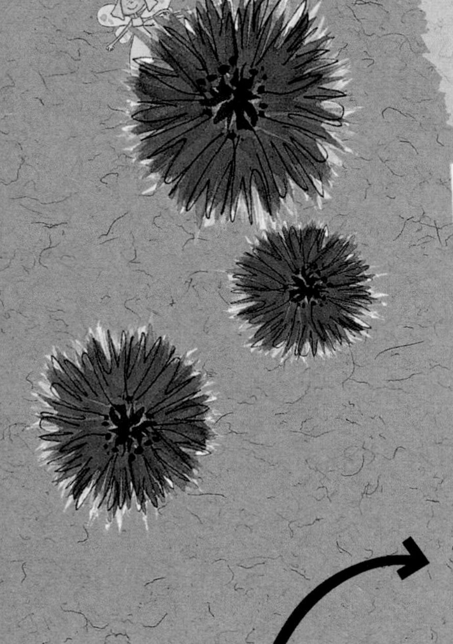

Pile these high on a pretty plate!

Princess Cornflower's Pink Meringue Kisses with Rose Cream

What you need:

Meringue

a little butter for greasing the paper
2 egg whites (ask a grown-up to separate the eggs for you)
125g/4oz/generous ½ cup caster sugar
1 small drop of pink food colouring

Filling and decorations

small pot of double cream,
2 drops of rose water (available from most supermarkets or you could use vanilla extract instead)

What you do:

Ask a grown-up to turn the oven on to 140°C/275°F/gas mark 1. Lay greaseproof paper on two baking trays and smear with butter (or use two silicone mats if you have them).

Ask an adult to help you whisk the egg whites with an electric mixer for about 3 minutes or until they are quite stiff.

Keep whisking while you add the sugar, 1 dessertspoon at a time until your meringue looks like little shiny mountains. Next add the pink food colouring and whisk again until the meringue turns pink.

Place teaspoon-sized blobs of meringue onto your trays (I used a piping bag so they look just like little kisses), leaving space in between them, and get a grown-up to put them in the oven. Bake for 1½ hours.

When they're done, ask a grown-up to take them out of the oven, then leave them to cool. Whip the cream with 2 drops of rosewater and sandwich two meringues together with the whipped cream to make a delicious 'Kiss'. Repeat with all the meringues.

Makes 48 meringues or 24 kisses.

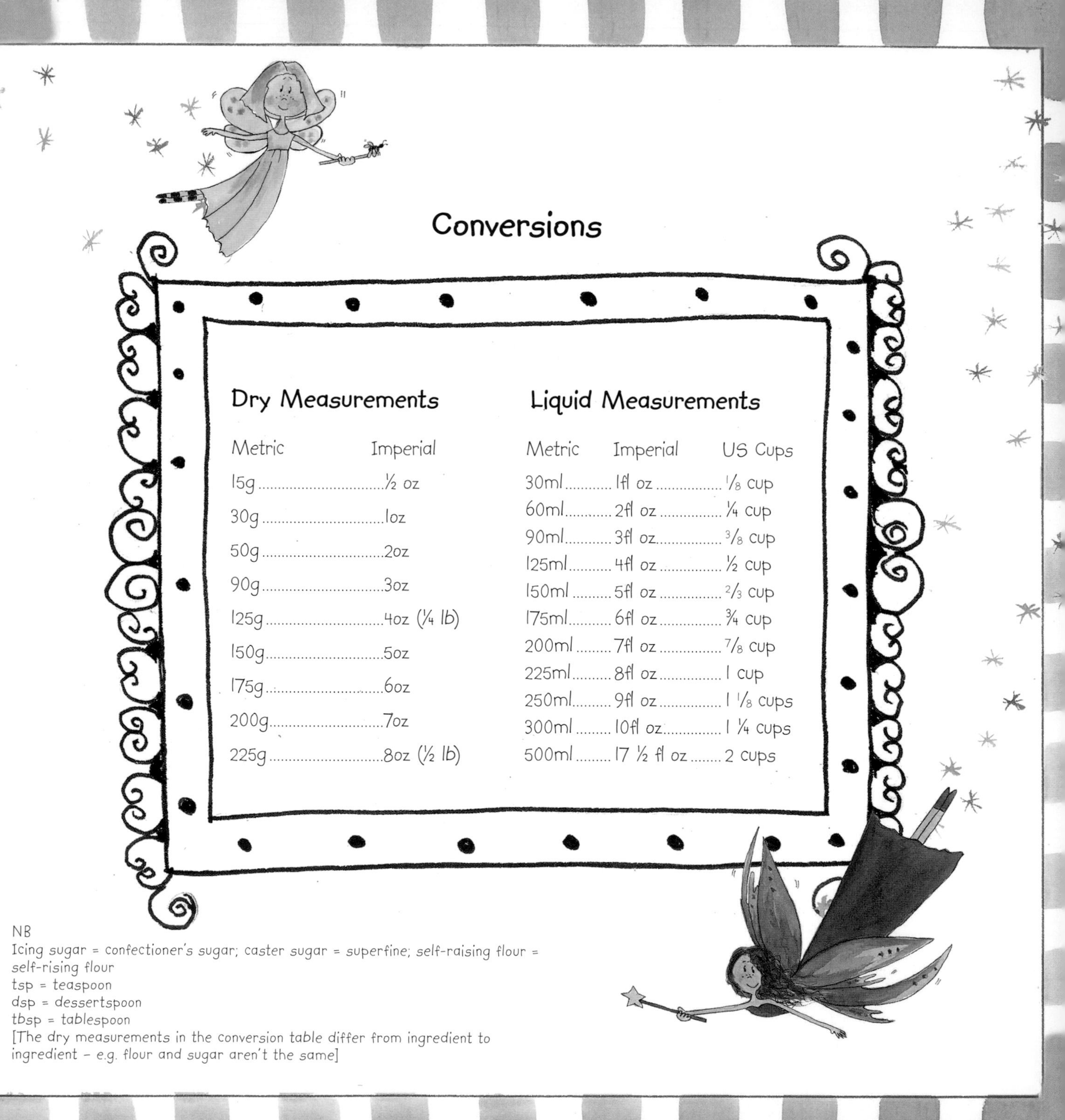

Conversions

Dry Measurements

Metric	Imperial
15g	½ oz
30g	1oz
50g	2oz
90g	3oz
125g	4oz (¼ lb)
150g	5oz
175g	6oz
200g	7oz
225g	8oz (½ lb)

Liquid Measurements

Metric	Imperial	US Cups
30ml	1fl oz	⅛ cup
60ml	2fl oz	¼ cup
90ml	3fl oz	⅜ cup
125ml	4fl oz	½ cup
150ml	5fl oz	⅔ cup
175ml	6fl oz	¾ cup
200ml	7fl oz	⅞ cup
225ml	8fl oz	1 cup
250ml	9fl oz	1 ⅛ cups
300ml	10fl oz	1 ¼ cups
500ml	17 ½ fl oz	2 cups

NB
Icing sugar = confectioner's sugar; caster sugar = superfine; self-raising flour = self-rising flour
tsp = teaspoon
dsp = dessertspoon
tbsp = tablespoon
[The dry measurements in the conversion table differ from ingredient to ingredient – e.g. flour and sugar aren't the same]

Here are a few helpful baking tips that I wanted to share with you...

1. Wash your hands before you start baking - fairies don't like germs.
2. Mum says it's healthier to cook with natural ingredients because they're better for you.
3. It's a good idea to wear an apron so you don't get too mucky. (Billy says he can't see the point!)
4. Always ask a grown-up to put things in and take things out of the oven for you.
5. Licking the spoon and bowl is yummy, but it is dangerous if you have used raw eggs. If you smile sweetly, you might be allowed to lick the icing bowl after you have finished decorating your fairy cakes.
6. If you enjoy cooking, always help to tidy up. My mum gets really cross if I just run off and play before everything is clean and tidy. (Washing up can be quite fun really!)

Acknowledgements

Team Flossie seems to be growing and I'd like to thank:
Polly and the team at Anova, Araminta and Philippa from LAW, the brilliant Nicole from Creative Acts, Sarah and Ruth from Renshaw Napier.
Not forgetting Kevin and Mark who have a particular love of fairies!
Special thanks to Carol, Biffy who makes me laugh and and is a wonderful baker last but not least the beautiful Tana!

Honey
Crystal
Minty
Candy

If you want to find out more about Flossie Crums and the fairies from Romolonia, visit

www.flossiecrums.com

Here you will also find extra recipes and my online shop for specialist cake decorations.

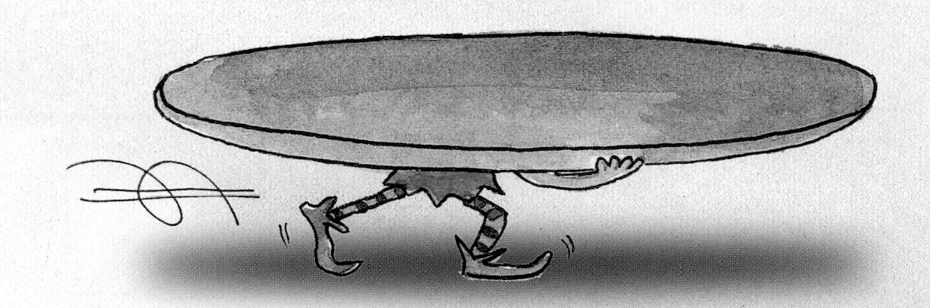